Paddington

the
Artist

First published in hardback in Great Britain by HarperCollins Publishers in 1985
First published in paperback by Collins Picture Books in 2000
This edition published by HarperCollins Children's Books in 2009

1 3 5 7 9 10 8 6 4 2

ISBN-13: 978-0-00-664745-4

Collins Picture Books is an imprint of HarperCollins Children's Books.
HarperCollins Children's Books is a division of HarperCollins Publishers Ltd.

Text copyright © Michael Bond 1985
Illustrations copyright © R.W. Alley 1998

Visit our website at: www.harpercollins.co.uk
Printed and bound in China

MICHAEL BOND

Paddington
the
Artist

illustrated by R.W. ALLEY

HarperCollins *Children's Books*

 One Sunday Paddington was out for a walk with his friend Mr Gruber, when they came across some paintings tied to the railings outside the park.

"It's what is known as an Outdoor Exhibition," said Mr Gruber. "They have one here every week when the weather is nice."

"All the paintings are for sale," Mr Gruber
explained. "This one is called 'Sunset in Bombay'."

"I'm glad I don't live in Bombay," said
Paddington. "It might keep me awake
all night."

"How about this one then?" said Mr Gruber.
"It's called 'Storm at Sea'."

Paddington suddenly wished he hadn't
eaten such a big breakfast.

"I feel sick," he said, and he hurried
on to the next picture.

"This is a picture the artist painted of himself," said Mr Gruber. "It's called a self-portrait. I think it looks very like him."

Paddington gave the picture a hard stare.

"I don't think I'll buy any paintings today, Mr Gruber," he said.

Paddington looked very thoughtful as he made his way back home to number thirty-two Windsor Gardens.

When he got there, Paddington collected all
his paints and brushes from his room and
went out into the garden.

The next Sunday, when he and Mr Gruber
had finished their walk, Paddington led the
way back towards Windsor Gardens.

"I'm having an Outdoor Exhibition of
my own this week, Mr Gruber," he said.

"This is meant to be a sunset in Windsor
Gardens. Only it took me quite a long time
and it got dark before I could finish it.

"And this is a picture of a rainstorm, only
it got very wet and all the paint ran."

"This is my best one," said Paddington. "It's a picture of me. I've put my special paw mark on to show I painted it myself."

Mr Gruber gazed at Paddington's portrait for a long time.

"It is very good, Mr Brown," he said at last, not wishing to upset his friend, "but I think you look even better in real life."

"I kept going upstairs to look at myself in the mirror," said Paddington, "but by the time I got downstairs again I'd forgotten what I looked like."

"Painting isn't as easy as it looks," Paddington added sadly, "especially with paws. I think I might give up."

"I hope you don't do that, Mr Brown," Mr Gruber said thoughtfully.

After Mr Gruber had said goodbye, Paddington sat down beside his paintings hoping that someone would stop and buy one.

But it was a warm day and no one came past.
In the end Paddington fell asleep.

Paintings
for sale -
Please pay
bear

When he woke up, Paddington found to his surprise that all his pictures had gone.

But tucked inside his duffle coat he found an envelope with his name on: Mr Paddington Brown, 32 Windsor Gardens. And inside the envelope there was some money and a note saying 'Thank you'.

If Mr and Mrs Brown recognised Mr Gruber's writing they didn't say anything. They hadn't had such a peaceful time for ages.

And best of all, Paddington carried on painting. So everyone was happy.

"I think I may paint a family portrait now," said Paddington. "That is, if I have enough paint left for all the smiles."